THREADS *of* DESTINY

DR. FISNIK "NICK" DEMAJ

Cover image © Fisnik Demaj
Interior Images © Fisnik Demaj with CoPilot

www.innovativeinkpublishing.com
Send all inquiries to:
4050 Westmark Drive
Dubuque, IA 52004-1840

Copyright © 2024 by Fisnik Demaj

Print ISBN: 979-8-3851-5681-8
eBook ISBN: 979-8-3851-5682-5

Published in the United States of America

Contents

Story Behind the Story

This story unfolds in the rough center of the small southeastern European country of Kosovo. It is here that my journey of life commenced. However, this story is neither about me nor the land of my origin.

The story begins in Radac, my village surrounded by towering mountains. Radac could have been a much more charming village; even as a child, I felt that the village was dull, and my life in the village was uninteresting because I lived a long way from the nearest town, which was about seven miles away.

The village, albeit peaceful, was frequently cloaked in darkness. Due to the poor maintenance and aging infrastructure, the lights would flicker and fade as if playing a cruel game, leaving the dwellers in a darkness that lasted for hours, sometimes even days. My entertainment choices at night were watching TV on one of the three available channels, playing chess with my father, having a guest, or reading a book. The nights the lights went out and the house was cloaked in darkness, it felt a bit scary. My father's excellent storyteller skills made those nights unforgettable. While the world outside stood in dark-ness, my father transformed our living room into a haven of en-chanting tales. His storytelling prowess was legendary, weaving narratives that transported me to realms far beyond the moun-tains that cradled our village.

My father, a man of few words but a symbol of strength and silence, bore the marks of labor on his hands, a charac-ter of his tireless service at a sugar plant since his youth. His quiet presence commanded respect, not just within our home but throughout our close-knit community. My mother's hands, worn from caring for us, would find solace in her lap as my father's words wove magic through the air. During these black-outs, my father's stories became my guiding stars, lighting the way through the uncertainties of life. As a child, I would secret-ly hope for the lights to falter, not just to escape the monotony of the never-ending news on our only television, but to bask in the glow of his captivating stories.

Since then, I always wanted to be a storyteller. Due to the de-cade-long war in former Yugoslavia, I came to California, USA, as a war refugee in 1999. I was 23 years old and spoke no English. When I had my own children, I purchased many children's books and read to them every day. However, most of the time, my old-est child did not like the stories in the books, so I improvised. I started making up stories simultaneously, and he loved my sto-ries. I opened the books, and based on the pictures, I made up my own stories, pretending to read them from the book.

The story you will read is one I only told my sons when they were tiny enough to sit in my lap; they probably do not remember it now. This tale stands out: a story that etched itself into the fabric of my being, shaping the contours of my dreams and aspirations. It is a story about great fortunes, missed opportunities, and demise. As you delve into the chapters of this book, you will discover how the flickering lights and my father's stories became the lanterns guiding me through the intricate tapestry of my existence, painting a portrait of a life shaped by the glow of familial love and the strength drawn from the shadows.

Radac, Kosovo (my birthplace)

Part 1

The Struggle

Today is my 18th birthday, Bato thought, and there was no one to celebrate him. As he gazed at his deteriorating home, he felt lonely and unhappy. He lacked friends, family, and love. He had nothing to live for, nothing to look forward to, nothing to be thrilled about.

He wondered why life was so harsh to him; was this all luck, future? As a young boy, he imagined a life where he could follow his dreams, make a difference, and be happy. The reality, however, was brutal and cruel. He needed more education, skills, contacts, money, and luck.

Bato knew he had to change his life but did not know how. He had tried many times before but always failed. He had sought guidance from friends and family but was disappointed. He had prayed for a miracle, but it was unanswered. He felt like giving up, but he refused. He prayed for a sign of what to do. Finally, he decides to speak with the village elders. "You are the luckiest man in the world," said one of the elders. How surprisingly gazed Bato. He had a spark of hope in his heart, a voice in his head, a vision in his eyes. He wanted to change his life and was determined to do it.

It would be best if you journeyed to the Mountains of the Sun. There, you will find answers to your prayers and guides for your future. Bato has never heard of the Sun Mountains. "What is in the Sun Mountains," asked Bato. "Sun Mountains are our most sacred mountains. Our people have been praying to those mountains for centuries; that is where our ancient gods live, my boy," one of the elders softly said.

The elders told Bato to take the journey to the Mountains of the Sun and ask the Gods directly about his future. The journey is long and treacherous, but in this journey, you will meet the most enormous fortunes a man has ever encountered. Bato decided to take a leap of faith and do something he had never done before: leave his village for the first time. He packed some belongings and left everything behind. He begins the journey of traveling to the sacred Mountains of the Sun.

Part 2
The Journey

There was never a time when Bato did not dream of seeing the world outside his small village. It is his wish to discover what his true destiny is and to fulfill his life's purpose. It was said that ancient heroes had found their guidance and strength in the Mountains of the Sun, heroes who performed great deeds and found great fortunes. It inspired him to embark on his own quest in their footsteps. The following day, he packed his bindle with food and other necessities, such as a map, a knife, and his flute, a gift from his grandfather. He slung the bindle stick over his shoulder and embarked on his journey. He knew it would be a long, treacherous road but was ready for any challenge on his very own adventure.

The Alpha Wolf

Bato was a few weeks into his arduous trek to seek knowledge of the fabled gods who lived above the rugged Mountains of the Sun. The expedition was lengthy and dangerous. Bato walked through impenetrable forests, raging rivers, and steep slopes. From severe weather to deadly wildlife, he encountered various hurdles. Nonetheless, his determination was unwavering. He was spurred by the desire to see the Sun Mountains gods, whose knowledge was claimed to be capable of saving him as they had many more before him.

Bato came into a strange scene a few weeks into his travels. In the middle of a snowy clearing, he came across an alpha wolf, beautiful, powerful, mute, and defenseless. The wolf had lost his howling voice and could no longer command his family. The pack was in chaos, fighting to endure the severe winter without the leadership of their leader.

Despite his dread, Bato felt sympathy for the silent alpha wolf. He remembered stories from his village about human-kind and wolves coexisting together. He decided to approach the wolf and listen to his worries.

Bato sensed the alpha wolf's deep comprehension as he peered into his eyes. He began to speak, his voice booming through the silence of the jungle. "I am on a journey to seek the wisdom of the legendary gods atop Mountains of the Sun," Bato claimed. My life has been difficult, and I am determined to find a solution. Bato spoke about his difficulties. He told the wolf about his adventures along the road, the obstacles he overcame, and the lessons he learned.

The wolf listened closely, never taking his attention away from Bato. His eyes were filled with admiration for the bravery needed for a young lad to embark on such a risky quest. The tie between Bato and the wolf became more assertive, their fates interwoven in their shared sense of responsibility and purpose. The wolf attempted to howl into the darkness again, echoing Bato's determination.

The alpha wolf looked at the young lad with adoration and sadness. Bato, you have been a true friend to me and my pack, he remarked. I wish I could accompany you on your voyage to the Mountains of the Sun, but I have a responsibility to fulfill. I am the leader of my pack and responsible for ensuring their survival throughout this extreme winter. They depend on me, and I cannot let them down.

"But there is something I would like to ask of you as a favor," the alpha wolf said after a little pause. When you meet the gods, kindly ask them about my howling problem. Let the Gods of the Sun Mountains know that I lost my voice in a fight with a rival pack protecting my family and how it hampered my communication with my family pack. Is there anything I can do to restore or improve my howling? It would mean a great deal to me and my pack.

Bato grinned, overcome with appreciation and adoration for the alpha wolf. "Of course, my friend," he said. I will happily ask the gods about your troubles, and on my way back, I will bring news for you. You have been tremendously kind to me, and I want to thank you in any way I can. You are an excellent leader and a wonderful friend."

The alpha wolf smiled and nodded. "Thank you, Bato," he said. You have a kind heart and a courageous attitude. I am honored to call you a friend. May the Mountains of the Sun protect and guide you. "Goodbye, my friend."

The Warrior Queen

Bato resumed his journey with fresh vigor. Days into this journey, he encountered a defeated army of a battled queen. The Warrior Queen, Elira, stood in the middle of the old forest, where the leaves murmured long-lost secrets and the moonlight carved silver pathways. Her kingdom was a tapestry of bright green hills guarded by warriors who bore her name.

However, darkness crept across her land. The wicked king and his entrenched army from a distant nation want her lands, including the rivers, orchards, and magic. His warriors, dressed in obsidian armor, marched toward her fortress, their flags aflame with the symbol of a black dragon.

Elira's throne chamber smelt of cedar and defiance. Her trusted sword rested on the marble dais, its blade crafted from fallen stars. Her counselors murmured caution, encouraging her to compromise and concede. But Elira's veins surged with warrior blood. She would not bow.

Every night, Queen Elira would climb the castle tower. She prayed to the old gods when the moon showered her in silver. She called for strength, wisdom, and a miracle. At that very moment, she saw a young man curled up, sleeping on the streets of her city. She orders her guards to bring him to her court. "Who are you, and what are you doing sleeping on the street in my city," asked the queen. "Please forgive me, I am passing through your city; tomorrow morning, I will resume my journey," Bato replied. I am going to the Mountains of the Sun to speak with the Gods about my missed future and lousy luck. Bato told the queen about his travels and encounters on his journey.

The battled queen told Bato that her luck had not favored her, and she was on the brink of losing her kingdom. Bato told the queen that she would get an answer from the Sun Mountains. The queen had been widowed for nearly two years since the king had fallen in one of the battles. Bato promised the queen that he would ask the Gods of the Sun Mountains about the queen's troubles. The beautiful, battled queen told Bato she would love to accompany him to the Sun Mountains, but her kingdom was threatened, and it would not be wise for her to leave the kingdom in turmoil. The next day, Bato continued the journey, resupplied with new clothes and plenty of food from the queen.

Bato continues the journey for a few more weeks. Near the endless wheat field, he saw an old man sitting quietly.

Childless Wealthy Man

A magnificent mansion in the middle of endless wheat fields, where marble statues whispered secrets and chandeliers danced with crystal tears. Despite his wealth, his heart bore an abyss more profound than the ocean's depths. Bato thought to himself, what troubles could a man of such magnanimous wealth have? Why would a man of this much fortune appear so despondent?

The old man and the boy spoke for many hours, told each other their life stories, and enjoyed each other's company. The old man told Bato his old age was catching up to him, and he had accumulated enormous wealth and fortune, but he had not been blessed with a child to carry on his richness and legacy.

He became depressed and sorrowful when he thought of himself dying and everything else dying along with him.

After a much-needed rest and gaining a great friend, it was time for Bato to continue his journey to the Mountains of the

Sun. The old man asked Bato for a great favor. "When you reach the Mountains of the Sun and speak to the Gods, would you ask about my worries and if there is a solution to my predicament? I wish I could accompany you to the Mountains of the Sun to directly bring my concerns to the Gods, but with my frail health, I would burden you," cried the old man. Bato assured the old man that he would deliver his message to the Sun Mountain Gods, and on the way back, he would have his prayers answered. Both said their goodbyes with hopes of meeting each other again.

A month has passed since Bato separated from the old man, and his journey has been treacherous, full of danger and novelties of adventures. Finally, Bato reached the Mountains of the Sun. Getting there took much work. The boy met many interesting people and creatures who had various problems on this expedition. Many people and animals he encountered had much bigger problems than he did. Nevertheless, he pressed forward with his endeavor to reach the Sun Mountains.

The journey took nearly a year, and he finally reached the Sun Mountains. He explained to the gods of the Sun Mountain the reason he took his treacherous journey. Bato was surprised to learn from them that he was the luckiest young man they had ever spoken to, and on his journey back home, his luck would strike many times; however, he must recognize the signs on his way back. He thought that was what the village elders also told him, but he had yet to find his luck, fortune, and destiny, even though he heard it for the second time. Aside from his personal problems, Bato also discussed the problems of his friends he had met on his journey to the Sun Mountain Gods. They spoke of the Alfa Wolf and his voice, the Warrior Queen and her defeated army, and the old man who did not have children of his own to pass his fortune on to the next generation.

Part 3

The Journey Back Home

After a few days of rest at the Mountain of the Sun, happy and excited, Bato began his journey back home.

A few weeks into his journey back, Bato had his first rendezvous with the wealthy old man with no children to share his wealth and great fortune. Excited and happy, Bato told the old man that he had delivered his message to the Gods of the Sun Mountain. "The Sun Mountain Gods said you must adopt as your own child the first young person you meet upon receiving this message and leave your entire fortune to him," said Bato. "If that is so, then you are the first young person I see, and I would like you to be my son and take over my fortune after I depart from this world," said the old man. I am sorry, but I must decline your offer because the Sun Mountains Gods told me I was the luckiest man, and my luck and fortune await me in my journey returning home. "I am very disappointed and heartbroken that you are declining my offer," said the old man. The old man wished Bato a safe journey back home and to find his fortune upon his arrival home. Bato said his goodbyes and left the old man heartbroken because he refused his offer to be his son. Nevertheless, Bato was ecstatic about his future and the message he received from the Sun Mountain Gods.

A few months into his journey, Bato entered the territory of the Warrior Queen, whose army was being overpowered by the neighboring kingdom, and her reign was in jeopardy of ending in tragedy. At the front gates of the queen's palace, Bato requested to speak with the queen and told the guards that he had brought great news from the Sun Mountain Gods.

"I delivered your concerns to the Sun Mountain Gods, and they said that you are in luck," Bato told the battled queen. "The gods said you must have a husband, a king, to lead your army, and you must marry the first man you meet after you receive this message to become your king and the chief commander of your army," Bato alleged. You are the first man I met, and I want you to be my husband, my king, and the chief commander of my armies," the queen replied. Yet again, Bato declined the queen's offer. The Sun Mountain Gods told me that I am the luckiest man in the world, and my luck and fortune are waiting for me on my journey back home," replied Bato. The battled and heartbroken queen reluctantly said goodbye to Bato, and they went their separate ways.

Bato continued his journey back to his village, convinced that his fortune awaited him at home. He had no reason not to think otherwise; the Gods of the Sun Mountain told him so. Happy and cheerful, he continued his voyage. As he got closer home, Bato had one more message to deliver to the Alpha Wolf, who lost his howling voice.

A few weeks later, Bato arrived near the territory of the Alpha Wolf. Approaching the wolf's den, Bato recognized the Alpha Wolf and explained to the wolf that he had reached the Sun Mountains and had spoken to the Gods, and he received great news for the Wolf, who could not howl to his pack.

The Alpha Wolf, anxious and excited, asked Bato, "What message have you for me from the Sun Mountain Gods?" "For

you to get your howling voice back and to howl to your pack, you must eat the first person you see upon receiving this message," said Bato. Alpha Wolf looked at Bato and said, "You are the first person I see after I received the message. Therefore, I am going to eat you.

Alpha Wolf devoured Bato, and its voice and the ability to howling came back.

The End